I0764571

I Know What

God Said

Part One

Shanetria Peterson

I Know What God Said

Unless otherwise indicated, all Scripture quotations are mostly from the King
James Version of the Bible.

Published by (Lulu Publishing)

Printed in the United States of America

ISBN: 978-0-6151-5630-9

DEDICATION

This book is dedicated to all those in the body of Christ that are

waiting for their future spouses. Though it may seemed to be delayed, it's certainly not denied! If God spoke it; it shall come to past. Don't give up hope for God will bring your investment to completion! There will be a bonus ministry teaching at the end of this book, and also, look for a possible part 2 in the near future! God bless!

Special Thanks to my parents Pastor Earl and Evangelist Jacqueline Williams...

My Angel: Shania,

My sister and brother-in-law: Galen and Tiwanda Hollingsworth

My two brothers: Earl Jr. and Timothy Williams

and a very special friend that I hold dear to my heart...

B.L.S.

Other Great Books By Author Shanetria

Now It's Time for Deliverance

The Greatest Part of Me

From the Smoky Mountains of Sevierville Tennessee: Pure Life Stream Devotionals for Women

I'm Not Going to Be Less than the Woman God Has Called Me to Be

On the Road to Destiny Ministry Writings of Youth Minister Shanetria Peterson

What He Want May Not be What He Needs

I Know What God Said Part II

Marriage God's Way

Prologue

"I don't understand this!?" Calise exclaimed to herself. " I wonder why after all of this time did I have a vision about Josiah Cunningham?" Shaking her head in disbelief, she pulled herself out of bed and immediately fell to her knees. She lifted up her voice and prayed audibly. "Dear Father, thank you for another day that you have made." "Thank you for the activities of my limbs and touching my eyes and behold they came open to see a brand new day." "Lord, thank you for my baby and my family." God I must ask you, what are you trying to tell me about Josiah Cunningham?" "I feel your presence in this room so strongly right now." "Help me to understand this dream and what it is that you will have me to do "Lord God, just when I was starting to be content in my singleness, I have this vision about Josiah. I know that I'm getting off subject, but Lord I need to understand what

All of this means. I ask all of these blessings and other blessings in Jesus most precious name I pray this prayer, amen.Note:

Habakkuk 2:3 For the vision is yet for an appointed time, but at the end it shall speak, and not lie: though it tarry, wait for it; because it will surely come, it will not tarry.

Chapter One

The church was brimming with people praising God to "We Worship You." Calise led her four year old daughter to her sister that sat on the second bench and went on up to the pulpit. She greeted all those that were already seated and took her place on the right side pew. She wore a silver two-piece skirt suit topped off with silver shoes with tiny silver diamond buckles on the side. Her hair was twisted in the front and the back flowed in beautiful straw curls her stylist Shan ice took her time and did the day before yesterday. Once settled, Calise laid her bible on the seat and stood up and began to sing along with the choir. *"Lord you are good and your mercy endureth forever." "Lord you are good and your mercy endureth forever." People from every nation and tongue from generation to generation. We worship you... hallelujah, hallelujah. We worship you, for who you are.* Calise lifted her hands in the air and began to praise God as the Holy Ghost moved upon her.

She closed her eyes and moved in the presence of the Lord. She had attended Holy Ghost Temple every since she was a child and there wasn't ever a time that she went and didn't feel God move in the building. Her dad, who was the pastor, preached the unadulterated truth and didn't compromise for a living soul. She was grateful for her parents who instilled holiness in her siblings and herself from children on up, but when she became a teen-ager, she strayed away from the pathway of the Lord to pursue after her own fleshly desires. Experience allowed her to become sexually promiscuous and rebellious. Her parents never gave up on her while she walked in sin; but instead, they kept lifting her and the rest of their children up in prayer believing for a change to take place on God's timing.

Calise eventually hit rock bottom when she became pregnant at age twenty-five causing her to drop out of college to focus on being a young un-wed mother. Through her guilt and shame, she managed to get on welfare and face the condemning eyes and the whispers behind her back, but she did not let people keep her from fulfilling her goals for herself, her daughter, and for the Lord. After Adrian was born, Calise went back to college and finished at the top of her class with a business degree in Accounting and Business Administration. On top of that, she acknowledged her call into the ministry by the prompting of God. Her calling was confirmed by her parents and a few others from her church. She was very active in youth ministry and with the help of the Lord, her peers, and her parents, she started an outreach that specialized in street, prison, radio Internet, and food ministry. Global Outreach also did conferences and seminars that emphasized focus on today's hottest issues in the Christian community.

The Lord delivered her from the harsh condemnation of others the biggest condemner being herself and used her to help other young people discover their purpose and role in the body of Christ. Calise was proud of the woman that she had become and the growing child that she was raising alone with the help of her family and the Lord. Adrian's father was not involved in her life, though he would send an occasional child support payment and pay a visit here and there, he never called nor did he help to raise her. The two had broken up before Adrian was born. Calise thought that she loved Harry when she had first met him, so after only three months, she moved in with him in the hopes that he would marry her. While living with him, she suffered emotional abuse terribly and there were many times that she sat at home alone on weekends while he went out to party with friend's sometimes not even coming home at all. He never called while he was out there in the streets and she didn't know if he was dead or alive when he would leave and not come home. Finally, when enough was enough, she got out of that horrible bondage, moved back home with her parents. They did not tell her, "I told you so," but instead they embraced her with open arms and have been by her side every since. Throughout her pregnancy, Calise was depressed on and off.

There were times where she would cry and it seemed as

though the tears would never quit pouring, but she knew she had to be strong for herself as well as for the baby that was growing inside of her. Eventually, as time went along after Adrian was born; Calise managed to put her life back on track, and allowed God to begin the healing process from that broken relationship. Harry wasn't the only bondage that Calise was caught up in, before him, there were several others and on weekends, she went and did strip shows for extra money to have while she attended college. That time in her life was the most embarrassing and humiliating encounters that she had. She remembered the lustful eyes of men that watched her every move. She went home with a man that she barely even knew and he got her drunk, took her to a hotel, and the rest was history.

When she awoke the next morning, she was left alone lying in bed without any clothing on. Her hands were cuffed where she couldn't move. After discovering what was taking place, she began to sob terribly.

After the realization of what had taken place set in, the man put on his clothing and left her in the hotel room to fend for herself. After that encounter she quit stripping altogether and that's when she met Harry. Calise surely didn't have a past to be proud of, but once she gave her life over to Jesus, she sought her deliverance from every single bondage that she had ever gotten entangled in. There are times where she would began to think about all of those things that she had been through. But she started rebuking the devil by the word of God and only by his grace she continues to press her way to be all that he would have her to be.

Calise sat down as the secretary began to read the announcements. She skimmed the crowd glad to see all of the familiar faces that had showed up at Church today. All of a sudden, she saw a very familiar face that she hadn't seen in awhile. Her heart began to pound loudly in her chest as her mouth began to water profusely. "I know that's not who I think it is…" she thought to herself…but as she focused clearly, Josiah Cunningham came into her peripheral view. She immediately thought back to the dream that she had of him and she couldn't believe her eyes. In the dream she had saw the three of them: her, Adrian, and him at a nearby park. The three of them were laughing and Adrian was sitting on Josiah's lap. Being careful not to stare as to cause suspicion to rise in anyone, Calise arose and immediately retreated

out of the side door. She rushed to the back and out the back door to catch air. She let out a whoosh and put her hand on her head to gather her composure. She said a brief prayer, repented for being distracted and

walked back into the church. While making her way to the front she silently questioned God: "Could it be that this with Josiah is about to transpire?" Her only answer was a small still voice that answered: “*Be still and know that I am God*.”

Chapter Two

Josiah Cunningham opted for the back row of his old home church, but instead decided on the fifth bench on the left hand side where the pew was empty. "Hopefully no one can smell cigarette smoke on me." He thought to himself. His friends followed him in tow each toting bibles. "Man this service is banging up in here." Danny Josiah's friend said. The way he said here sounded like ear instead of "here." Josiah grinned and whispered, "It's has always been like this up in here." The way that he said here also sounded like ear as well. Josiah left Holy Ghost temple when he began college nearly five years ago. He moved away from Louisiana to take up residence in Houston, Texas.

He was a diligent follower of Christ before he left and went to college. When he made it there, he discovered there was plenty of temptation to fall into. He got caught up into running women, smoking, and partying. There were times that he would feel guilty and he immediately fell on his face before God to repent. He would do good for a little while but eventually he always went back into the same old lifestyle. He was home for the weekend visiting his mom and she insisted him and his friends to attend church that particular Sunday. Josiah graduated college at the age of twenty-one. Upon graduation, he opened up his own construction business in Houston.

Cunningham and Son's was extremely successful and he had no one to thank but God for that. Two of his friends helped him to run the business and with their diligence and credentials, they drew in over one-hundred and fifty employees. Life seemed to be good for him at the present moment. He had his on and off again girlfriend Lisa Wells, who lived with him on weekends, he had his business, more money than he could handle, his Lexus, his friends, and of course, his family…but one thing that was evidently missing from his life and that was his spiritual depth in God. Josiah was extremely handsome maturing quickly from the little boy with the squeaky voice to the stocky man with a now booming masculine voice. His hair was low cut and wavy and he stood nearly 6 foot and 3 inches tall in height. His warm chestnut skin was flawless. A small goatee was growing around his mouth that he kept neatly trimmed.

He knew he looked good and loved the fact that women from all walks of life were attracted to him. He looked around at the familiar faces in his old church and smiled. It was good to be back home although the last place he thought he would end up is back at his home church. It wouldn't have been so bad if he didn't have to face Pastor King. Maybe, he would leave early or soon as church let out, he would try to make a hasty exit to avoid greeting him. Over the years, Pastor King had been his spiritual mentor and the father that he never had.

Although his dad was still living and was still married to his mom, he had never been there to instruct him on becoming a man. His mom did much of the raising and Pastor King took up the slack of being his spiritual guide as he began to walk with Christ. There was more hurt than a little bit that took residence in his heart but being the macho man that he was, he wasn't the type to wear his heart on his sleeve.

There was a deep longing in him that he knew could only be filled by God, but the problem was he just didn't know how to totally surrender his all to Jesus without sacrificing all that he had accumulated over these last few years. The secretary stood up to the podium to make announcements and that's when his eyes fell on the beautiful young lady in the pulpit. "Oh man!" He thought to himself. "Mom did tell me that Calise was ministering!" She grew more beautiful every time that he saw her.

He couldn't help but stare at her as she fumbled with her hanky. She glanced in his direction and her eyes seemed to linger on him. He read the shocked expression on her face in seeing him in the congregation. After she stared for a few seconds, she abruptly got up and went out of the side door. Josiah's heart sank. He remembered all too well what everyone had thought at one time. There were many at Holy Ghost Temple that thought that she would make him a good wife. Hearing the word wife scared him then as it scares him now. Lisa was a potential prospect physically wise, but she wasn't what he needed spiritually. She always begged and wined for him to buy her things, and never took not having intercourse for an answer.

The two had been through their share of ups and downs, and somehow he felt that he was stuck with her. He was not sure why because he was confused with the words lust and love. She was a beautiful woman, that wasn't the problem, but he just didn't see her as wife material. His mom pressed on the subject of marriage and often threw hints about marrying Lisa, but he would always brush her off and change the subject. He just wasn't ready to make a hasty move in marrying and then find out that the person he said, "I do" to was not indeed the woman that God intended for him to spend the rest of his life with. Seeing Calise today stirred some strange emotions inside of him. He knew that she was strong spiritually and had gone through some bad experiences in her life.

He looked over to her four year old daughter that was sitting on her auntie's lap. He smiled and marveled at how beautiful and big that she had gotten. He felt deep down inside that Calise would have made him the perfect wife, but he couldn't imagine the fact of being with someone that he had grew up with in the church all of his life. He wasn't ready to commit to anyone like Calise who he felt deserved royalty and not someone who wasn't sure of his soul's salvation. After a heart warming sermon from Pastor King, and communion, church was dismissed for the day. Josiah stood up and prepared to make his hasty exit but was immediately surrounded by people that he hadn't seen in awhile. Bombarded by hugs, and kisses on his cheek from the elderly women, he forgot totally about not wanting to face Pastor King. He felt a strong tug on his shoulder all of a sudden. He looked back and true enough, it was Pastor King standing there grinning at him. "Hey Pastor, how's it going?" He said. Pastor King greeted him and they embraced. "How have you been holding up?" Pastor King asked. Josiah paused. "I can't lie to you Pastor; my walk has not been what it could be in the Lord." Pastor King smiled. "Thank you for being honest with me." He said.

"I know that you are caught up in some things that God is not pleased with." Josiah hung his head. "Yes, Pastor, and it's totally eating away at me too." He replied. "Won't you give me a call before you leave to go back to Texas?" Pastor King said as someone came up to him preparing to greet him. "I will." Josiah said clutching his Bible to his chest. He made his way out of the door with his friends on his heel. "I wonder what he has to talk to you about." Danny said. "Man, you know Pastor King been my spiritual mentor for some years now." "There ain't nothing that I can hide from him that he don't know." "Everything that he tells me is all based on God's word." "I can go in there and find whatever he tells me in there." "I know he a true man of God and everything he tells me, I know it's in that Bible."

"He going to scold me, but when he scold me, he always pray with me and encourage me to seek repentance and allow God to cleanse me." "He always tells me that I'm a leader and not a follower." "Man, I just want to find my way back to God." Josiah said as he walked toward his car. Danny agreed and fell into step along side of him. While walking across the parking lot, he saw Calise walking over to her car that was parked next to his. She was holding her daughter's hand as they walked. She looked over to him and waved. He waved back and prepared for conversation. They met upon each other at almost the same time and his friends whistled in approval.

Josiah ignored them and gave Calise a big hug. "It's been a

long time Josiah." She said. Josiah reached down and gave Adrian a hug too. "Yeah, it's been a very long while." He said as he stood back up. Calise was about 5 feet and 4 inches so he had to look down at her to talk. Josiah then introduced her to his friends. Calise shook their hands and told them that it was a pleasure and a blessing to meet them. The group of men were amazed at the word of God and

wisdom that poured forth from her mouth as she talked about how much she loved and adored him. Upon finishing, she gave each one of them a Gospel tract with her phone number on it and told them if they ever needed prayer or spiritual guidance, to call her. She hugged Josiah one more time, put her daughter in the car, and looked at him one more time before getting in the car and driving off. "Man that is a dynamic woman of God right there!"

Danny said. "And she's beautiful too!" Josiah's other friend Steven said. "Yep." That's Calise. Josiah said as they all got in the car. "Man it's so coincidental that you were parked by each other today." Danny said staring suspiciously at Josiah. "Man what are you implying?" He asked. "I saw the way you looked at her man." He said. "Boy you throwed!" Josiah said laughing. "Calise is like a sister to me." He said pulling into church traffic.

"Yeah, that's what you mouth say." Kenny, Josiah's other friend said from the backseat. "Man won't yall stopped ganging up on me." I have known Calise all of my life just about and just because we shared a few words today don't mean nothing!"

"There's nothing there for her." I got my woman so just shut yo mouth…" Joshia's friends chuckled and dropped the conversation before it turned into a frivolity controversy. They then went into a new conversation about rims, but Josiah was silent. He couldn't understand why he felt a strong connection toward Calise. "It's nothing man…" He thought to himself, but his heart screamed contrary to his thoughts…

Chapter Three

Calise was extremely shocked that she had seen Josiah today. She clutched her hand tightly on her steering wheel as she waited patiently for traffic to move along. Adrian was in the back seat quietly playing with her dolls. Josiah was still extremely handsome, but she noticed a vague difference about him. His lips were slightly darkened giving a tale-tell signs that he smoked. "He's truly different from the Josiah I remembered." She thought to herself moving along with the escalading traffic. Calise's mom smiled at her knowingly when she saw him talking to her dad. She couldn't believe that nearly the whole church once thought that they would make the perfect couple.

"We are extremely different." She thought to herself and besides, "I'm three years older than he is." Calise pulled up at her parent's house still deep in thought and parked beside her sister's SUV. She got out of the car and got Adrian from the backseat. "We're at grandma's house!" She shouted cheerfully as she took off running to the door. "Honey walk on that concrete before you fall!" Calise explained, but Adrian charged ahead. Calise shook her head and walked behind her daughter to the door. As she neared the entrance, the smell of baked chicken hit her nostrils. She smiled warmly. She was extremely famished from not eating all day. The King's always cooked Sunday dinner for their children and anyone else who wanted to come by and get a plate. There were many from the neighborhood, that usually stopped in to grab a bite to eat before going on their way, but today, it was only the family that took up residence in the King's spacious home. Calise entered the door at the sound of laughter. Edward King was sitting on the overstuffed sofa poking fun at Calise's sister, Brenda about not cooking for her husband. Derell, Brenda's husband was sitting on the loveseat across from his father-in-law hooting with laughter. "Hey, yall don't gang up on Brenda now." Calise said in a playful mode as she took a seat at one of the bar stools in the kitchen. "She be trying." Edward looked at his youngest daughter and said, " Neither one of yall ain't trying hard enough." "Yall come here and eat every Sunday!" "You can't feed a man hot dogs everyday and expect to keep him." Pastor Edward concluded as he let out a hoot of laughter. "Oh dad, cut it out." Brenda said going to the stove to check the chicken. Calise's mother came out of the backroom with her apron on. "Are yall up in here cutting up?" She asked with a hand on her hip and a playful smile on her lip. "Awwww…there she goes!" Pastor Edward said rolling his eyes playfully. "I have you know, taught my daughters how to cook now if they don't do it that's on them!" She said laughing.

Calise laughed and got off the stool to get a glass of water. Adrian climbed in Edward's lap to watch television. "Where them two knuckleheads at? Calise asked referring to her two brothers. "They in the back room watching that football mess." Calise's mother said with a shake of her head. "Audrey, if you don't mind, pour mc somcthing to drink."

Pastor Edward said. She immediately went to the cupboard and took down a cup to pour her husband some juice. Calise and her sister Brenda resembled their mother greatly with their big brown eyes, long hair and high cheekbones. Audrey was a dedicated woman of God, who stood beside her husband in the ministry. She was extremely wise beyond her years. Gray speckled her black hair and slight wrinkles outlined her mouth. She was extremely beautiful and encouraged her daughters to keep themselves up especially since they were growing older. She taught her daughters the meaning of being and living the role of a virtuous woman. Calise was extremely thankful for the guidance of her mother and her grandmother who was now deceased.

Brenda wore her hair straight while Calise wore her's either in straw curls or natural. Calise's brothers took after their father. Terrance and Terrell were both tall cocky and handsome just like their father. Terrell was light skinned while Terrance was dark. Each had cold black wavy hair, long slender noses and mustaches. Terrance was the oldest being twenty-three and Terrell was the youngest of the bunch being the age of eighteen.

Terrance and Brenda were the only two that were married. Terrence's wife April worked on Sunday's so he spent most of his time at his parents house or out with friends. Terrell was still dating his high school sweetheart Patricia Haddon. Calise was the only one that didn't have anyone at the particular moment. Being in the ministry and standing firm on God's word intimidated potential suitors, but she was determined to follow Christ and to wait on nothing less but his best for her and her daughter. Audrey picked up on her youngest daughter's quietness. "It was good seeking Josiah today." She said, causing Calise's face to turn beet red. She looked up at her mom and saw the smile playing across her lips. "Yeah, it was nice seeing him." She said nervously flipping through a Brylane Home Magazine uninterested in its contents. "He has grown quite successful too," Brenda said moving on side of her mom. "Yeah, he's really doing well for himself." Calise said with a yawn.

"That boy will make you a fantastic husband when God gets

through with him." Audrey said, moving to the stove to take out the chicken. "Mom, come on, don't start playing the match matching game." Calise said still flipping through the magazine once more. Pastor King piped in. "I got to talk to him about some things first." Calise hated when her parents talked over their children's head as though they weren't even there. She shook her head and jumped up from the stool for the second time. "Okay, let's eat." She said, busying herself in taking down plates.

Brenda shook her head and smiled. They all stared at her and then back and forth at one another, but she paid them no mind. "Wow, maybe I should bring Josiah up all the time." Audrey said, because any other time, you will sit on that bar stool and not move!" Calise laughed and began putting the plates on the table. "Why is everyone trying to put me with Josiah?" She thought to herself, they were so different, but yet, she felt a strong connection to him that she couldn't understand. The family gathered together, Calise did a prayer and they all ate until they couldn't eat another bite. Afterwards, they enjoyed a dessert of Lemon Cream Pie. Around seven o' clock, Calise gathered Adrian in her arms said her good-bye's and prepared to go home. She lived three miles down the road from her parents. Upon getting home, she laid Adrian down, went to her room, got out of her Sunday's best, took a shower, read her Bible, prayed and watched a little television. After watching the news, she then retreated to bed. The nights were getting extremely hard for her for that was the time loneliness seemed to creep in over her. She didn't understand why she felt the need to cry. She truly missed companionship but wasn't about to do anything irrational to fill the void that she felt. She was grateful for God being there with her in her deepest hour of loneliness. She still couldn't understand why she had that strange dream of her, Adrian and Josiah. "It's really a coincidence how I saw him today." She thought to herself. "Lord, I don't have all the answers to this, but I trust that you do." Calise said to herself, with that thought, she fell into a peaceful sleep.

***

The drive to Houston had wore Josiah completely out, upon hitting his pillow, he waited for sleep to hit him, when it didn't he sat up slightly punched it and lay back down. Lisa was sound asleep on the side of him. He was extremely tired of letting her share his bed when he knew that he had no intentions of marrying her. He didn't understand why he couldn't get Calise out of his mind. Seeing her today awoke the strangest feelings within him that he just couldn't explain. He didn’t want to become an emotional roller coaster, but he couldn’t shake the feelings that stirred within him at the mention of Calise’s name or if an image of her filled his mind.

He loved her smile, the warmth that it brought to the lives that she touched including his very own and he didn’t deny that she was a prize to be gotten, but she just wasn’t “his prize.” This was the first time that he was intrigued by a woman without having sexual thoughts cloud his brain. Calise was a rare jewel and she deserved nothing but the best. "I just don't see her as someone that I would be with." He thought to himself. "She's not my type, we're totally different breeds, but why can't I stop thinking about her?" Josiah thought. "This is madness!" Josiah felt Lisa's hand on his back. For the first time, he cringed. "Is everything alright baby?" She asked him. "Yeah, I'm fine." He said gruffly, but deep down inside he was confused as to why thoughts of Calise was running through his brain even though he had his girlfriend lying on side of him. He turned his back toward Lisa and attempted to fall asleep onc morc time, but instead of sleep, his mind still filled with thoughts of Adrian and Calise instead. "I think I need a cigarette." He said to himself jumping up to go to get his pack off of the dresser. He took one out, lit it and took a long drag. As he blew smoke out of his mouth, he began looking out of the window. "I really got to quit this habit." He said to himself, "this is not who I am.

" Lisa stood up and walked over to him. "What's the matter honey, you rarely smoke at night." She told him. "I'm fine." Lisa smiled and stood on tiptoes to kiss him fully on the lips. Josiah put out his cigarette and they went back to bed. "Other things could wait." He thought to himself, "but right now, life was going too good to sacrifice all that he had. He had to put Calise out of his mind and concentrate on his life. He had the business, a fine woman to share his bed with, more money than he could handle, a nice house, a car, and his family. What more could he ask for?

Chapter Four

Calise took off her warm up suit and slipped into some pajama's being that she had the house to herself tonight, she didn't have much else to do. Adrian was spending the night at Brenda and Derell's house to give her a break. Calise checked her answering machine and skimmed quickly through them. The messages mostly were from ministers that were interested in booking her for conferences and seminars, but she stopped dead short on one recognizing the voice as Josiah's. "Hey Calise, I will give you a call later, I have some things that I want to ask you about." He said hastily. Calise smiled to herself. "What on earth can he want with me?" She thought to herself. She remembered the tracks that she had handed to him and his friends the week before. She concluded that maybe he wanted to discuss something about it. Whatever the case, she would find out when he called.

She cooked an omelet, poured her a glass of juice and sat down. Just when she was nearly finished, her phone rang. Thinking it was her sister giving her an update on Adrian, she hastily picked it up. "Hello?' She said into the mouthpiece."Hey how's it going Calise." Came the husky voice on the other end. It was Josiah. "Oh, hi Josiah!" She exclaimed. "I thought it was my sister calling to give me an update on my baby." "She's spending the night over at her house. "Oh yeah?" Josiah questioned with a chuckle. "Yes." Calise said. "I saw where you called me earlier." She said getting to the core of wondering why he was calling. "Oh, yeah, I wanted to ask you a few things about the Bible." He said. For the next twenty minutes, they discussed the Bible and Calise answered each question that he had. Since their conversation went smoothly, she felt the need to share the vision that she had about him, her, and Adrian. She told him all the details of it and afterwards there was a long awaited silence. "Gee, Calise, I don't know what to tell you about that." He said. "It was just a dream." He concluded. Calise's heart sank. "Yeah, maybe it was." She said quietly. "The truth be told, I already have a girlfriend and we are happy together." He added. "I have all that I need and I don't think life can get any better than this." Calise sat down on her couch to gain her composure. "Yeah, you're right." "Adrian and I have all that we need too and since God is the head of our lives, he will supply all of our needs according to his riches in glory."

"Well, since I've answered all of your questions, I need to be going now." They said their good-bye's and hung up the phone. Calise sat rooted in her spot for a while longer before getting up.

Tears welled in her eyes, and spilled down her cheeks. She angrily wiped at them with the back of her hand. "Well, that went well." She said out loud. "Josiah was surely right, that was indeed just a dream that I had." "Now, I've made a complete fool of myself in front of him." She added. Calise was extremely embarrassed about what just transpired. She got down on her knees and prayed while tears poured from her eyes. Rejection was something that she always had to deal with mostly all her life, but leaning on Jesus always brought her through. Now a fresh wound was birthed, but she was determined to allow God to heal it. Never again would she let another man take away her smile and her self-esteem. "Now, I know that there is nothing between Josiah and me and that there could never be anything between us, I will put him out of my mind and go on with my life." She wasn't totally convinced by what she thought, but at the moment she rationalized with what she felt. "I won't let being rejected get me down." She said standing up to dust herself off. "I'm ready for change!" She said as she went to the mirror. The first thing she wanted to do was change her hair. She plugged up her flat iron and took her time to flat iron each strand straight.

***

Josiah sat on the deck on the back of his house. He felt extremely guilty for what he had told Calise. He sighed, took out a cigarette and smoked it. He didn't usually smoke at night, but lately all he could think about was Calise and Adrian. He couldn't understand why he felt so drawn to them. He thought back to the dream that she told him that she had. The truth be told, he had a similar dream about them, but didn't dare bring that up because he didn't believe in dreams or that God can speak to people through visions. Hearing her last words stung his heart... *"Adrian and I have all that we need too and since God is the head of our lives, he will supply all of our needs according to his riches in glory." "Well, since I've answered all of your questions, I need to be going now."* "Well, I just told her the truth and if it hurts, then so be it." He thought. He was not sure if he heard hurt or anger, or both in her voice, but whatever the case, it was no concern of his. He got up and walked back into the house still deep in thought.

He and his friends were going out to a club that night. He saw that Lisa had arrived and heard the water running in the shower. She was preparing to go to the club with them along with two of her other friends who were also girlfriends to his two best friends. After checking himself in the mirror, he walked the little ways down the hallway to the bathroom. He opened the door and went in. Lisa yelped with excitement when she saw him. Josiah forgot all about the incident with Calise and instead focused on Lisa. "Yeah, this is the way that it's supposed to be." "Just me and my lady." He happily said to himself.

Chapter Five

After a month Josiah attended Holy Ghost Temple once again. He was surprised to see Calise's hair straightened out. She wore a light pink and yellow dress that stopped above the knees. She was indeed beautiful and he couldn't help but to stare. Adrian wore a pink and white ruffled dress and all of her hair flowed down her back. She bore a great resemblance to her mother, grandmother and auntie. She went to the first bench and climbed in her grandmother's lap. Calise was preaching today, so he could hardly wait to hear what the Holy Ghost had given her to say. When it was time for her to speak, she opened her mouth boldly and did a brief praise and worship session to usher in the spirit so the word would have a free course. Josiah was drawn to his feet and for the first time in ages, he began to praise God.For the last three weeks, God had been dealing with him strongly about the sin in his life.

He hadn't picked up a cigarette since the week before last. He strangely didn't have the desire to have one. Lisa and his friends were noticing the changes that were taking place in him. He started picking up his word more, praying again, and asking his home away from home pastor about the word of God. He strongly felt the presence of God in his life and when he would try and resort to old habits, strange things would come up. One night he had prepared to go to a party, but had a bad nose bleed before leaving out of the door. On his way to the store one day his tire blew out in the middle of traffic almost causing the cars behind him to slam smack into him. The business was suffering a great loss due to employees leaving to go to the new utility plant that opened in Arlington. The assets of his company were swiftly decreasing and if he didn't see where money was going, pretty soon he wasn't going to have enough money to pay his employees their pay. His guys got paid every other week instead of every week, and at the rate that they were going, he would probably have to start paying them every two weeks something he wished that he wouldn't have to do considering the ones that have only one income coming in their household.

He came home stressed and perplexed because of his job. He

and Lisa started arguing more for all she seemed to care about was partying, having intercourse, and whining for him to buy her something new. Eventually, he had to sit down and talk with her and they both decided that it were best that they both went their separate ways. After he let Lisa go,He felt that God was knocking on the tables of his heart, but he still didn't know how to open up to him. At the same time, he still felt such a strong connection to Calise stronger than it had ever been and he knew deep within himself, even though he wouldn't admit it, "that she was indeed the woman that God had chosen for him." After the praise and worship session ended, Calise asked the congregation to turn their Bibles to Romans the 6th chapter. She looked around the crowd and stood a little ways from the podium with the cordless microphone poised to her mouth. "It's good to see some familiar faces in the crowd that I haven't seen in awhile." She said.

"I didn't know what I was going to preach on today, but the Lord lead me here to Romans the 6th chapter." "I don't know what your idea of grace is, but just because it's there for the taking doesn't give a one of us an excuse to keep on sinning!" Amen's flooded through the crowd. "Jesus paid the ultimate price for our freedom, and some of us are using our freedom to do any and everything that we are big enough to do and then when the going gets rough and tough, here we come trudging in to the house of the Lord." "Something wrong somewhere when we are governed more by our flesh than we are by our spirit!" Amen's flooded through the crowd again. Calise then read through Romans the sixth chapter and then flipped over to Galatians the 5th:13-26th verses. She then preached boldly by the power of the Holy Ghost on the differences between the flesh and the spirit. Josiah was convicted by her message. After Calise was finished, the doors of the church were opened. Surprisingly he got up and went to sit in one of the chairs. Calise avoided looking at him but told everyone to stand on their feet and praise God for allowing him to come.

Josiah's mom, Mrs. Joann Cunningham was completely in tears at seeing her son rededicating his life back to God. After two more people came up, Calise went down and took their names.

Pastor King came out of the pulpit and hugged him. Josiah couldn't help but start crying a little bit. He was allowed the chance to say something, and so he told a brief part of his testimony. When he was finished, the church applauded for him and began to praise God. One of the mothers of the church got up and came over to him. She hugged him long and hard and told him. "That's good son." "God shoul got a great work for you to do."

"You see that young lady right there?" She asked him quietly pointing at Calise. Pastor King allowed the other two candidates to say a brief word while the mother talked privately to Josiah. He followed Mother Hubbard's finger to Calise. "Yes, ma'am. He said. "That's the woman that God has to help you in what you are going to be doing for him. She's chosen by God and so are you." "Been praying and asking for a wife, and there she is right there." She added. Mother Hubbard walked away leaving him completely shocked. Josiah held his breath and let it out slowly. He knew that word from Mother Hubbard confirmed what he had been feeling in his heart. He knew Mother Hubbard for years and knew that she was truly used by God. Josiah stared at Calise and she stared back at him. She walked over to him and gave him a hug. "Congrats brother and welcome back."

She told him turning to leave. "Calise wait." He whispered to her. She turned on her heels and faced him. "This is not the right time Josiah." She whispered. "There's so much doubt between the two of us let God work things out in his perfect timing." She added. Josiah clamped his mouth shut to keep from saying anything else. Calise walked away and went back into the pulpit. Josiah didn't take his eyes off of her. He wanted to know what she was thinking and how she was feeling. Mother Hubbard's words echoed in his mind as he took his seat. This was all so much to digest.

He knew what Mother Hubbard said to be the truth but for months he ran from it, he tried to put it out of his mind. Also for those last months, his thoughts were constantly on Adrian and Calise. He knew that he couldn't walk any farther without letting her know, that he "knew," that God had chosen her for him and no matter what it took, he was determined to make her his wife. He felt that God was definitely trying to tell him something if he would just open up his ears to hear. Church let out and many people young and old came around to congratulate him. He clutched his Bible tightly and happily thanked them. Pastor King hugged him tightly and patted him on his back. He was able to have a long talk with him and receive the guidance that he needed.

Pastor King gave him words of wisdom and enlightened him that he had a strong calling on his life and that there were boundaries up where he couldn't even cross because of the covering that God had over his life. Pastor King also ministered to him on the subject of deliverance and he told him that when you're chosen out by God, eventually, you will have to surrender because nothing will go right until you do. Pastor King indeed was right because things were beginning to come at him left and right that he couldn't even began to explain and map out. The church was nearly cleared out, but Calise lingered behind to talk to one of the lady Evangelist's. He walked toward them and patiently waited for them to finish their conversation. Evangelist Johnson congratulated him for rededicating his life back to God and retreated out of the side door. Calise stared at Josiah indecisively. Her lower lip trembled as tears threatened to pour from her eyes. There was so much doubt and apprehension running through her mind. Adrian ran up to them and Josiah gave her a big hug. "Hey sport." He said. "Hey." Adrian said grinning from ear to ear. "Are you going to be my new daddy?" She asked startling both of the adults. Josiah laughed slightly. "Let's leave that up to the Lord shall we?"

He said. "Mommy, I'm going to go on and get in the car with Auntie Brenda and Uncle Derell." Adrian said. "Okay." Calise replied. "We're going to go on to dinner at ma-ma and pa-pa's house." She added. "Good, then we can go together since Pastor and Sister King invited me over." Josiah said. Calise sighed defeated and grabbed her coat. "I caught a ride with Brenda and Derell, this morning so I guess they just knew I would be going home with you." She said in a slightly cold manner walking out of the side door leaving him to follow. Josiah clicked the alarm off button on his keychain, unlocked the door to the car and opened the passenger side so Calise can climb in. She got in and he closed the door behind her. He walked around to the driver's side and got in. "Calise, I'm sorry for the way that I behaved that night I called your home." "I don't know what came over me." He said. "Josiah, you were just being brutally honest." "You admitted that you had a girlfriend and that you were happy with the way that your life was." "Maybe those weren't your exact words and how you meant it, but that's surely what it sounded like to me." "Thank you so much for being honest." "Adrian and I do not need anyone who's not honest trying to *intrude* in on us." "I've had enough of that." Josiah let out a whoosh and started his car. "Calise, the last thing that I ever want to do is to hurt you." "I feel that I can't be the man that you and Adrian need." "I mean look at my life?" "Look at all the things that I have gotten myself in?" Calise laughed. "Josiah, welcome to the real world." "When we play into the devil's hand and let him play tug-a-war with our flesh and our spirit, that's how we get into sin way over our heads." "We allow him to tell us that a little sin is okay and that since we have accepted Jesus as Lord and Savior that we can do anything that we want to do." "That's the farthest thing from the truth." "Just accepting Jesus as Lord and Savior is just step one." "We need to allow God to deliver us from the bondages of the enemy and to sanctify us daily." "We are not our own, we were brought with a price, so therefore we should glorify God in our body, and in our spirit, which are his."

"We don't have a right to continue in sin because grace is there for the taking." "I know God led me to preach that sermon today for a reason." "Yes, he did Calise." Josiah said, turning the corner. "Calise, I'm not perfect, but if you allow me to get my act together, I'll show you that I can be the man that you and Adrian need." Calise looked over at him. "Josiah, if you try in your own strength, you will not be that man because whatsoever is not of faith is sin. When we learn better, we are required to do better." "You can't overcome any addiction in your own strength. God takes us through a cleansing and renewal process, but we must allow him to work that process in us and have faith that he that began a good work in us will bring it to completion." Josiah sighed. "I have been trying to do things in my own strength, but little by little God has been breaking me down." "Yes, he will break you down Josiah, it may be painful, but the outcome will be far above what you could ever ask or imagine." "You are right." Josiah said. They drove the rest of the way to Calise's parent's house deep in conversation.

Whey they arrived, they got out and retreated to the house still in conversation about the Bible, before entering behind Josiah, Calise gave up a brief prayer of thanks to God. "I did what I felt that you wanted me to do dear Father, now the rest is up to him." She said. "Thank you for allowing my questions to be answered."

Chapter Six

Over the course of the next few weeks, Calise and Josiah grew closer together. Although there was closeness something was missing. Josiah seemed to be a bit distant. She couldn't figure out why he seemed so withdrawn, but she quietly observed him without bringing it up. He drove from Texas every other week to church services and to spend time with them. He was in his home town for a whole week and decided to stay in a hotel in Calise's

neighborhood. They were riding along the highway on their way home from Opelousas. Josiah exhaled and stretched his legs out as he held the steering wheel. Is everything okay Josiah?" Calise asked. "You have been exceptionally quiet." She added. Josiah didn't take his eyes off the road. "I'm fine." He replied. Adrian sat in the back seat playing to herself. "I don't buy that."

Calise said dusting the stray crumbs that fell from the funnel cake she had eaten. "Everything is fine." Josiah said looking at her briefly. Calise sighed and turned to look out of the window. "Can you turn on the radio?" Calise said. "It's awfully quiet in here since we're not talking that much." Josiah reached over and turned on J. Moss's latest C.D. They drove in silence a few miles down the road. Adrian and Josiah interacted for nearly an hour before there was total silence in the car. Calise looked in the backseat. Adrian was fast asleep. Calise smiled to herself and turned forward. She didn't know where things were going to go between Josiah and she but she prayed that things would fall in place for them. "There's something that's bothering you Josiah."

Calise said. "How do you figure that something is wrong with me?" Josiah asked sternly. "Hold up." Calise said. "I don't know why you are coping an attitude with me, but I did nothing to you." "If you want to harbor this childish behavior, then I will leave you alone to sulk." "Please just get me home and drop me and my daughter off ." “I don’t need drama Josiah.” With that statement, she scooted away from him until her body leaned against the door. "I'm sorry." Josiah said gruffly. Calise said, "Sure." They rode in silence for a long time before Josiah spoke. "Calise, I'm scared of what's going to transpire between us." He finally spoke breaking the silence. Calise looked over to him. "Scared of what?" She said. "Scared of what I'm feeling for you." He said. "What is there to be scared of?" She asked. "This is a totally new experience for me Calise." "I've never felt this way before."

He replied quietly. "Enlighten me Josiah because the last I knew we were just keeping things platonic according to you." She replied. "Well, I'm telling you now that the feelings that I'm having for you are more than platonic." He added. Calise was stunned not knowing what to say. "How long have you been feeling this way?" She asked him. "It's been awhile." He told her as he gripped the steering wheel. "Josiah, I feel the same way." "Let's just allow God to bring things together in his timing." "There's no reason to be afraid with God being at the head and center of our relationship." "I want to be able to give you and Adrian all that you deserve and more." Josiah, I'm not running away from how I feel about you." "I've ran so many times, but this time, I'm not running from this." Josiah reached out and grabbed her hand. An electric current shot through Calise for that was the first time that they ever touched in that manner. For the rest of the way they rode in silence as Josiah stroked her hand in his.

"Calise would you laugh if I told you that I don't know how to be in a relationship?" He asked her letting her hand go. Calise

looked at him fondly. "No, Josiah, that's not a funny thing." "When we've been hurt, misused, and have had our hearts broken numerous amounts of time, it's difficult to give your heart again." "When a relationship is truly ordained by God, it does seem truly like a new experience, because you are with the right person and you want to do the right thing to keep that person." She added. "You're right." "Just please be patient with me as God continues doing a great work in me." Josiah said. Calise grabbed his hand again. Josiah, if this is God's will for us, I don't have any say so, other than to cooperate and go along with the process.

Chapter Seven

Over the course of the next few weeks, Josiah and Calise experienced changes that they thought they would never face. There were many challenges that caused them to almost split up. Josiah's family along with Calise's family and outsiders all seemed to have a part in their relationship.

Calise was experiencing panic attacks from stress. She and Josiah would argue and not speak for days at a time, but eventually, they would began to miss one another and make amends.

The Lord had been strongly convicting the both of them to be still and realize that he was the author and the finisher of their relationship in spite of what was going on, he was the one that had the last say so. One day the couple had a big argument about rumors that were spreading that Josiah's mom did not want him with Calise. The couple didn't talk for three whole weeks because of it. At church Mrs. Cunningham stopped speaking to her and would give her an evil glare every time she saw her. Apparently, the rumors were true she realized after Mrs. Cunningham started treating her in this manner. Calise's parents told her not to worry about it but to move forward in the things of God and let God be God in her and Josiah's relationship. Calise had nothing but love for soul-mate's mother. After that particular argument and after making amends, the couple decided that they would never ever allow anyone else to come in between their relationship and cause them to be at odds with one another. One day, Josiah asked her about the idea of eloping. Calise was a bit hesitant.There are so many things between us Josiah."

"Our families will never understand why we would want to get married considering all the things that have taken place between us for the last couple of months." Josiah held her hand in his. "Our relationship is not perfect, but we clearly know that God want the both of us together." He told her. Calise smiled fondly at him. "Well, if you think that we will be okay, I've already thought of the prospect of marriage with you so what do we do about it?" With that particular question hanging in the air for a few hours, the two of them silently planned a get-away to tie the knot. Calise was afraid that maybe they were moving too fast, but realized that God's timing didn't have one thing to do with what their idea of timing was. Arriving on the white sandy beach of Nassau, Bahamas, where her wedding was to take place, Calise could hardly believe her eyes. The tranquil waters of the turquoise mass of rippling delightfulness of the Caribbean sparkled under the lazy, summer sun spreading her glory over the face of the deep waters. She had spent nearly four hours being dressed and pampered for her and Josiah's wedding. The perfume she wore captured delicately in her nostrils as a soft Caribbean breeze being to blow soflty across the beach. Her long wedding gown captured the sun's attention gleaming like a ball of cotton on a windy, sunny spring day. The dress was a sweetheart gown from Milano, Italy. It did not have any sleeves in it but it harbored a shapely beaded bodice and the skirt flared slightly from the waist. Instead of a viel, Calise wore a diamond beaded tiara. She was indeed beautiful. Her long hair hung in loose waves about her face. She smiled as she continued walking toward the arch where Josiah and a preacher with dread locks that were carefully pulled into a ponytail stood. In the background, a radio played soft music. When she got closer to them, she saw the look of approval on her husband to be and the preacher's face. A lone tear came out of her right eye but she wiped it quickly away and smiled. The two of them had been through so much and it was amazing that the both of them were standing there doing what so many other people in their lives said and believed that they would never do. Josiah looked extremely handsome. His white tux fit him perfectly giving his skin a radiant healthy glow. His goatee along with his mustache was neatly trimmed and his hair was neatly cut close to his head. When Calise arrived in front of him and the preacher, he asked them in his accent were they ready to begin. They both grabbed each other's hands and nodded. The preacher grinned and prepared to begin their ceremony. "You are so beautiful." Josiah told her staring at her dreamily. "You look wonderful yourself." Calise replied gripping her husband to be hands tightly. The preacher then begin the ceremony. When it came down to saying their vows, Calise went first: She looked deeply into his eyes and began: "Josiah, we have known each other every since we were kids." "I did not believe that you and I would be standing here today." "We're standing here because we believe in each other and we believe with all of our hearts that this is what God said." "I promise to love you through good times and in bad, in sickness, and in health, when all seems to go good and defintely when all is going bad, "I am here to be by your side, to coach you in the Lord, to hold your hand when you feel as though you can't go on. I'm here to stand with you until death do us part." Tears streamed down Calise's face as she finished her vows. Josiah took the back of his right hand and wiped them gently away..."My love," he begin. "I've never in my life thought an angel could walk the earth until I met you." 'I've never been so drawn to anyone in my life as I have to you and Adrian." "You are the wind beneath my wings lifting me up before God." "The warmth of your smile, the glow of your eyes, and the presence of your being fill me completely." "I promise to love you in good times and in bad, in sickness and in health, when times seem hard and rough, I'm here for you." "I'm here to aid in your vision and your dreams and together our dreams and visions will become one as of now." "I'm standing here today, because I too believe in us and I do believe that God saved you just for me. Yes, my love, I do believe with all of my heart that this *is* what God said." "I promise to love you until death do us part and even after death, our love will still hold a token that many people will use to fund for their love." After they said their vows and a prayer from the preacher, the two exchanged rings. After they said their vows and exchanged their symbols of love, the preacher then said, "Now you may kiss your bride." The two leaned closly into each other and for the first time, they shared a kiss...the magic of the touch of their lips captured the summer sun causing fire bombs to explode within one another. A gift that only husband and wife could share and it create a sensation that God approved. That's when the two THEN became one.

After their weekend trip to the Bahamas, the two came back happy to say that they were now husband and wife. No one else knew about their marriage, but they were preparing to break the news to all at dinner later on that evening. After unpacking their clothing and sitting down to a late afternoon snack, Josiah put Adrian to bed and came in and sat on the overstuffed sofa beside his wife. Calise was quiet. “Honey, you okay?” He asked her taking her in his arms. She sighed. “I’m just thinking of what everyone is going to say about us.” Josiah stroked her cheek. “It doesn’t matter.” He replied. “We don’t need anyone else’s approval but God’s.”

“If he be for us, who can be against us?” He added. Calise smiled.

"You're exactly right." She said. "After the weekend, we will be home in Tennessee, ready to start our new life together and either our family is going to have to accept us or not, but if they don't, then that's their problem." Calise smiled and closed her eyes. "I can't wait to go to Tennessee and start our life there." She told him. "Neither can I." "Adrian will truly love the atmosphere." Josiah added. Calise agreed. The two sat on the couch cuddled together and fell asleep peacefully in each other's arms.

***

Later on that night at dinner, Josiah and Calise sat side by side at Calise's parents dinner table. They both wore their wedding rings, but no one seemed to notice them. After a wonderful dinner with strained conversation, Josiah stood up and cleared his throat. "I would like to make an announcement." He said. "No one knew about their weekend get-away, so the news that he was about to break was going to shock them all. When he looked around at all that sat at the table, his mom blurted out angrily. "What do you want to say?" She said gruffly for she was thinking along the lines of him talking about a wedding. Josiah cut her off. "Calise and I went away for the weekend." He began…and we are now husband and wife." He said after a moment's hesitation. Gasps went throughout the room. A few of the couples siblings stood up and congratulated them. Josiah's mother and Calise's parents sat still. Mrs. Cunnigham stood up and blurted out. "How dare you do this to me Josiah!"

She exclaimed. "Why didn't you consult me first before you made the biggest mistake of your life!" She added. "Now, hold up!" Mrs. King said standing to her feet. "Your son hasn't made as much of a mistake as my daughter has." She began…the two were about to quarrel when Calise stood up.

"It was Josiah's idea to tell you all what we had did, but I was totally entertaining the idea of moving to Tennessee

with my husband first, before telling this, but now that the secret is out, it's a done deal and you all are going to either have to live with it or sulk, it's your choice!" "The three of us are happy, and Josiah and I feel that this is God's will for both of us

and we don't need your approval for God is our creator and we answer to no one else but him." "We say that we are Christians, but sometimes we have a strange way of behaving." "Why can't we just work together as brothers and sisters in Christ and resolve our differences?" "Yes, Josiah and I have had problems, but what relationship doesn't?" "We've both came a long way and we thank God for all that he has done for us." "Now, we're not going to leave here feeling bad if you don't accept us, so you have the opportunity to either accept or reject, but we're staying together." With that statement, Calise pushed back her chair and left the dinner table. Her parents followed her into the kitchen. She expected World War Three to break out but instead, her parents embraced her and congratulated her. Josiah came in the kitchen to check on his wife. He stopped in his tracks when his in-laws stopped and stared at him. The King's went up to their son-in-law and gave him a big hug. Josiah smiled at them both. "I'm not going to do anything less than take care of your daughter and granddaughter."

"I thank God for the precious jewels that he has placed in my hands and I know that jewels are delicate, so I'm going to treat them above the jewels that they already are." He added. "What I have in my hand is priceless treasure." The King's hugged him

again and left out of the kitchen. Calise smiled at her husband as he came up to embrace her. "I'm glad that you stood to say what you did." He whispered to her. They kissed lightly on the lips. "I have every right to defend us." She added. They exchanged light conversation and held on to each other a few minutes longer. Just then the kitchen door came open. Mrs. Cunningham came in and stood watching them. "You know?" She began looking at her son, "You know I don't have to accept this right?" She questioned. "Mom, you do what you want to do." "I love you with all of my heart, but I'm not responsible for how you feel. He added letting go of hishis wife and brushing past her to go out of the kitchen. Mrs. Cunningham turned and gripped his arm tightly. "You have made the biggest mistake that you could ever make!" She yelled. Josiah smiled. "Mom, the biggest mistake that I've made in my life was not discovering how much I loved Calise sooner."He said, pulling his arm out of her grip. "God loves and accepts us and that's good enough for us." He added, turning to walk away. Calise stood against the sink as Mrs. Cunningham stood

with her mouth open widely looking sternly at her daughter-in-law. "You take care of my child!" She yelled. Calise smiled, Mrs.

Cunningham, I don't intend to do any *less* than that because I live for God and since he is love and I'm connected to him, I have nothing but love for my husband who he has blessed me with." Calise said and walked out of the kitchen with her head held high.

***

That Monday, the Cunningham's put the remainder of Calise's and Adrian's belongings in their vehicle. Their family stood around them as they loaded up to go. "I'm sure glad, that God put the two of you together." Mrs. King told the happy couple. "Thanks mom." Calise said hugging her parents tightly before getting in their SUV. The moving trucks had already drove on before them. The King's hugged Adrian and placed her in the back seat and buckled her securely in. Tears welled in Mrs. King's eyes. "Mom, we're only nine hours away."Calise said with a wide grin. "Everything is going to be alright."

We are still going to drive down and help out with the ministry." She added. Mrs. Cunningham shook her head up and down. Josiah went around to hug his in-laws, and then made his way back to the passenger side. "Well, you all, we are going to go head

down this road." He said. Mrs. Cunningham hadn't talked to Josiah since Friday night. "What are you going to do about your mother?" Mr. King asked. "Oh, she'll come around." "She's just upset that I am not allowing her to run my life." Josiah said with a grin. "She'll be mad for a little while, but she'll come to terms with everything." Mr. King smiled. "Well, we're not going to hold you all up." He said backing away from the window. The two waved good-bye. Calise blew a kiss, Adrian began waving from the back. Josiah blew the horn and drove away. Once a way's down the road, Josiah broke the silence, "Can you believe that we are finally husband and wife?" He asked her. Calise smiled, "Yes, I can, because I know what *God* said."

She replied resting her head against the back of her seat.

Bonus Teaching:

The Truth that Men and Women Won't Face and the Issues that The Church Won't Talk About

We are living in a time where God's ordained order is being twisted, mocked, and where the enemy is trying and failing to make God's word out of a lie, but his days are numbered and they are few! It takes cooperation from the men and women of God to continue putting him to flight and whatever lie he's telling, we must tell and stand for the truth!

Most Men are refusing to take their rightful places, women are frustrated with the lack of support from men, and the church is too busy fighting so in turn, it leaves unfulfilled visions and dreams among believers.We all know the holy scriptures concerning marriage...we all have looked for months in (our ministry group Iron Sharpens Iron) at **5** starting at the **28th** verse of **Ephesians** and other verses pertaining to marriage. We know that God's word goes out in righteousness and it shall not return to him void.

Why are we running from God's word and order? Marriage is a sacred and holy union and it won't change from being what God has ordained it to be no matter what the world is saying and doing!Many people are afraid they are going to get hurt, many people are afraid of divorce, ect...but why not trust God? Well, maybe because as a body, we are afraid to do that as well. If we can't be trustworthy of our Lord and Savior Jesus Christ and if we can't walk by faith and not by sight, if we mistreat our Lord and our Savior then it's no wonder why we can't face our responsibility as men and women and come together in harmony instead of bickering to do what God has called us to do individually, as a couple, and as parents to our children.

Someone has to answer for the children! They are growing up in broken homes, they are being abused and neglected. They are hurting and bleeding inside...they are silently wishing for two parents to show them love instead of arguing and fighting with one another...Who's bold enough to take their rightful place?

Have we shrunk back so far from the arrows of the Devil that we have let his fear cloud our judgment and sit behind our selfish motives? It's time out for being self-centered! We have let our pride, our wants, our needs, and our desires cloud our minds hindering us from receiving and carrying out the instructions of God. The same God that we are trusting for everything else in the church, we should be trusting him to carry out the plan of our lives concerning marriage.

How beautiful it would be when men start accepting the wives that God has brought them, instead of going out and hand picking ones that don't even know the definition of a wife. How beautiful it will be when the wives start presenting themselves as such instead of seducers and giving away what the Lord has given to them for their husband...hmm...

I know what the Lord is depositing into this vessel won't be popular and accepted among many, but my yes, Lord meant so much to me and I will not back down from putting it out there. We preach on the same issues over and over again, failing to bring forth the entire word of God...and delving deep into the mysteries and wonders of God's heart...We can't get just the surface of his heart, we must get deep within his heart...

I can't preach just half of the issues of God, but I gives what the Lord gives to me even sometimes, it's a mouthful to swallow at times for even myself, but it's not about me...We have got to stop being so close-minded...We as women and men of God are suffering and instead of blaming the Devil, we are fighting one another. We are giving each other the silent treatment in relationships...instead of facing our issues like mature men and women, we sulk and act childish...What's wrong with the picture Saints?

I wrote a sermon a few months back about seeds of discord being sown...the Lord had given me that word early one morning and I woke up and posted it...that word surely did come to past...everybody mostly that I knew was going through something in their homes, among their families, among their spouses, and yes, right there among the four walls in the church...confusion broke out!!!

Like one of the Prophet says at our church: "All hell breaks loose when God speaks something to you."I can't speak for anyone else, but all hell broke loose in my life, but I know and still know that the vision did not lie and that my God has an appointed time for it to come past...We must not give up the fight! We will reap in due season if we faint not!

We have got to stop allowing other people to control our lives and our relationships. We must learn to bridle our tongues and if we know that it would hurt us, then we know it will definitely hurt others so the best thing to do is not to say it!

God did not call women to take on roles of both husband and wife...he didn't call her to rear up children alone, he called a man to walk by her side and aid in disciplining the children...the father is the biggest discipline counterpart in his children’s lives, and if he can't govern his own household, then how can he govern the house of God? Oh, come on and wake up here with me somebody...We need to get back on our faces before God and began to cry out...not just for the symptoms, but for the root of bondages to be lifted off of each other...women, we need to lift our husbands up to God in prayer, and men, we need you to lift us up to God in prayer...we need to pray together on one accord for one another and for our children! We must be their support system! Until we fall in line with the word of God and no I'm not just talking about

JUST that Holy Bible because God is speaking daily new statues and ordinances according to his word for his children to follow...it goes beyond the book. Somebody don't have that yet either, but that's alright...I pray it's gotten before judgment day...

We need to spend time with the Father so that when we emerge from his presence someone else can tell that we have been with the Father, and I'm not just talking an affair either, but a personal fellowship with our husband the Lord God! It should show upon our faces...the reflection of the father...

This teaching is not here to touch on the symptoms of issues, but it cuts to the very core...God called me to bring forth his heart to his people...and it can either be accepted or rejected...I love God too much to not do what he wants me to do...I want to see his word being performed just like he said in his word and I know it shall accomplish that what it's sent out to do!

Romans 1:16-3216

For I am not ashamed of the gospel of Christ: for it is the power of God unto salvation to
every one that believeth; to the Jew first, and also to the Greek. 17For therein is the
righteousness of God revealed from faith to faith: as it is written, The just shall live by
faith. 18For the wrath of God is revealed from heaven against all ungodliness and
unrighteousness of men, who hold the truth in unrighteousness; 19Because that which
may be known of God is manifest in them; for God hath shewed it unto them. 20For the
invisible things of him from the creation of the world are clearly seen, being understood
by the things that are made, even his eternal power and Godhead; so that they are without
excuse: 21Because that, when they knew God, they glorified him not as God, neither
were thankful; but became vain in their imaginations, and their foolish heart was
darkened. 22Professing themselves to be wise, they became fools, 23And changed the
glory of the uncorruptible God into an image made like to corruptible man, and to birds,
and fourfooted beasts, and creeping things. 24Wherefore God also gave them up to
uncleanness through the lusts of their own hearts, to dishonour their own bodies between

themselves: 25Who changed the truth of God into a lie, and worshipped and served the
creature more than the Creator, who is blessed for ever. Amen. 26For this cause God
gave them up unto vile affections: for even their women did change the natural use into
that which is against nature: 27And likewise also the men, leaving the natural use of the
woman, burned in their lust one toward another; men with men working that which is
unseemly, and receiving in themselves that recompence of their error which was meet.
28And even as they did not like to retain God in their knowledge, God gave them over to
a reprobate mind, to do those things which are not convenient; 29Being filled with all
unrighteousness, fornication, wickedness, covetousness, maliciousness; full of envy,
murder, debate, deceit, malignity; whisperers, 30Backbiters, haters of God, despiteful,
proud, boasters, inventors of evil things, disobedient to parents, 31Without
understanding, covenantbreakers, without natural affection, implacable, unmerciful:
32Who knowing the judgment of God, that they which commit such things are worthy of
death, not only do the same, but have pleasure in them that do them.

Second Bonus Teaching:

<u>It May Have to Die In Order for it to be Resurrected</u>

You may seem as though you're going around in circles. You may seem to think that everything that you try to accomplish for yourself crumbles and fall down.In this season, you may have lost your job or may be going through hell on it, your children may seem like they are getting worse instead of better, your health may seem like it's going from bad to worse and...your relationship may have totally crumbled and fizzled out right before your very eyes...so what do you do when everything that you think that gives you life dies? God has a purpose for everything.

Ecclesiastes 3 KJV

1To every thing there is a season, and a time to every purpose under the heaven: **A time**
to be born, and a time to die; a time to plant, and a time to pluck up that which is
planted; 3A time to kill, and a time to heal; a time to break down, and a time to build up;
4A time to weep, and a time to laugh; a time to mourn, and a time to dance; 5A time to
cast away stones, and a time to gather stones together; a time to embrace, and a time to
refrain from embracing; 6A time to get, and a time to lose; a time to keep, and a time to
cast away; 7A time to rend, and a time to sew; a time to keep silence, and a time to speak;
8A time to love, and a time to hate; a time of war, and a time of peace. 9What profit hath
he that worketh in that wherein he laboureth? 10I have seen the travail, which God hath
given to the sons of men to be exercised in it. 11He hath made every thing beautiful in his
time: also he hath set the world in their heart, so that no man can find out the work that
God maketh from the beginning to the end. 12I know that there is no good in them, but

for a man to rejoice, and to do good in his life. 13And also that every man should eat and
drink, and enjoy the good of all his labour, it is the gift of God. 14I know that,
whatsoever God doeth, it shall be for ever: nothing can be put to it, nor any thing taken
from it: and God doeth it, that men should fear before him. 15That which hath been is
now; and that which is to be hath already been; and God requireth that which is past.
16And moreover I saw under the sun the place of judgment, that wickedness was there;
and the place of righteousness, that iniquity was there. 17I said in mine heart, God shall
judge the righteous and the wicked: for there is a time there for every purpose and for
every work. 18I said in mine heart concerning the estate of the sons of men, that God
might manifest them, and that they might see that they themselves are beasts. 19For that
which befalleth the sons of men befalleth beasts; even one thing befalleth them: as the
one dieth, so dieth the other; yea, they have all one breath; so that a man hath no
preeminence above a beast: for all is vanity. 20All go unto one place; all are of the dust,
and all turn to dust again. 21Who knoweth the spirit of man that goeth upward, and the
spirit of the beast that goeth downward to the earth? 22Wherefore I perceive that there is
nothing better, than that a man should rejoice in his own works; for that is his portion: for
who shall bring him to see what shall be after him?

Today, I just want to focus on verse 2

"A time to be born, and a time to die; a time to plant, and a time to pluck up that which is planted;"

This verse doesn't just give revelation to the physical man...

There are relationships that may go into full bloom...and God may have showed you the outcome before you saw the beginning. Our beginning is God's end so keep that in mind. Your relationship may go into full bloom only to fizzle out and eventually die. God has an appointed season for ministry and we know that marriage is also a ministry right?At the appropriate time your relationship may be born once more and again in God's appointed time.

I pray that we realize that the vision has an appointed time. That appointed time is not your timing because everytime that you try to do it in your timing, it will fizzle out and die. God will get his glory out of every detail of our lives. I don't think many of us realize what we mean when we say yes, to God.That yes, means we fully understand.

Romans 8:28;"And we know that all things work together for good to them that love God, to them who are the called according to his purpose."

It also means that you fully understand, that the just shall live by his faith. We don't live by what we can see as children of God, but we live by what we don't see. When your relationship dies after it happend prematurely and you **KNOW THAT GOD** gave you that spouse, you must understand that it wasn't your timing and trust God to birth it forth in his timing.

You must in turn walk by faith and believe that it will happen in God's appointed time. You must believe that you must take your hand off of it...you must understand that you can't lean on your own understanding...you must understand that you will have no part in getting it back off the ground. but your cooperation is definitely needed. The well-renowned author and minister Derek Prince had to go through this with his wife Ruth Prince...they had no contact and no personal communication through the season that their relationship died. Their relationship personally did not really even began before it died right at birth. Although the pain was great, both trusted God that it would resurrect again if it was God's will for them to be again and in God's appointed time, it resurrected!In order for a relationship to be what God has ordained, it must be done God's way and not you or your spouses way...this is not really about you or your spouse, but it's about God and he will get his glory.

"Therefore, what GOD has joined..." (Matthew 19:6b).

God does not join together what he does not approve! Just because a couple marry doesn't mean that everybody is joined together under the same yoke and harness. God forbids gay marriages and we know he is nowhere in it! Only **HOLY** people can partake in a **HOLY** union and be joined together.

The Scripture that commands us not to pull apart "what God has put together" deals with "what GOD has put together!" If God did not put the marriage together, we shouldn't be in it in the first place. If we are in such a marriage, we can get out. IF WE WANT OUR MARRIAGE TO BE BLESSED BY GOD, GOD MUST APPROVE OF OUR MARRIAGE, otherwise, we will receive the very minimum amount of blessings from God, if any. If we do not repent but continue in our stubbornness, we *"are treasuring up for ...[ourselves] ...wrath ..."* (Romans 2:5). Then we wonder why God allowed this to happen? How did we get into this terrible relationship anyway? We blame everybody but ourselves.

So even if your relationship dies and it's God ordained, that doesn't mean that it's time for you to start looking again for a prospective mate, ect...unless God gives you the okay to be released from what he has spoken to you. We must understand that it isn't the season for your relationship, it doesn't mean that you go against him and try to grow it because whatever gets planted and it's not God's timing, it will be plucked up, but although it hurts...(yes, it can be extremely painful!) Trust God to work out the details for it and I promise you if you walk by faith and not by sight, when the relationship that died fully blooms again by the hands of God, it will be wonderful!

May God Bless each of you.

Third Bonus Teaching

Do We Still Believe?

Hebrews 11:1 **(AMP)** NOW FAITH is the assurance (the confirmation, [a]the title deed) of the things [we] hope for, being the proof of things [we] do not see and the conviction of their reality [faith perceiving as real fact what is not revealed to the senses].

Hebrews 11:1**(KJV)** Now faith is the substance of things hoped for, the evidence of things not seen.

Praise God from whom all blessings flow! Many of you are in line for a blessing and many of your blessings include the spouse that God has spoken to you...if not marriage...things are working in **YOUR** favor. This is for those that are walking in obedience and have been led to our ministry group. I started this group in faith and obedience to God when he alerted me that he was preparing me for marriage spiritually and let me know to also prepare physically and I answered his call. So many things have happened since that time, **(almost a year ago before our group Iron Sharpens Iron started)...**now things have came up that it takes a tremendous amount of faith to go through and believe the outcome that God promised me. Many of you have also experienced so many changes from last year up until now, but I want to ask you the question tonight: Are you going to continue trusting God or give up on him?

Giving up on God seems like the thing for many believers to do that have been trusting him for a promise for a long time, but Jesus didn't give up on us when we were walking waywardly, so we shouldn't give up on God. I know that may be easier said (or typed) than done, but if we allow God to preserve our spirits and give

us grace throughout each stage of our waiting on him, we will begin to endure until the promise. I don't know at this moment how things have shifted, but I do **KNOW** that they have shifted in my favor as he promised...the gap in between the time that this promise was spoken and until now, I don't know the events that's currently taken place in the spirit rim, but I know that God is doing a **NEW THING** and I'm confident that all things will work together for the good of those who are the called according to his purpose. It doesn't matter how uncomfortable we are, just know in the most uncomfortable time of your life, God will speak comfort to your spirit...so before you begin to worry and fret, God will come and give you rest...if you lay

awake at night and worry, God will come and put ease over your mind and you won't have any choice to go to sleep. Worrying haven't changed a one of our situations, but prayer does!

The book of Philippians 4:6-7 tells us;

6Be careful for nothing; but in every thing by prayer and supplication with thanksgiving let your requests be made known unto God. 7And the peace of God, which passeth all understanding, shall keep your hearts and minds through Christ Jesus.

So if God spoke a promise to you and told you to prepare for marriage...were you obedient or did you try to question and rationalize with God?Don't you know that questioning and doubting God will cost you a price? We are to have confidence in the Lord and we can't have confidence in the flesh, but it takes being in the spirit to be confident...our minds should be Christ like in every aspect. We may not understand why things are happening that seem as though it's against the promise. You and your chosen spouse may not have even met yet or you may have met and a relationship may have birthed off the ground and faltered, but if God said it then that settles it! If God made the world in less than seven days, don't you think that he is able to bring a promise to completion? You have to get him out of the box, stop worrying and fretting because you are not creating an atmosphere for him to come in and do his job. God is not bringing to completion something that has not already existed...and once our minds shift to the supernatural we will begin to see things God's way and rest in his presence...not saying that things will be comfortable always because of our fallen state, we will find ourselves in the flesh worrying, but when we begin to trust and lean and depend on Jesus we will find ourselves floating through the struggles and not leaning on mistrust and emotions to guide us through.

So tonight, I want to ask you: "Is your promise worth holding on to?" "Do you still believe that God has spoken that husband or wife for you?" God is going to get his glory in this situation and everyone around will **SEE** that this was a work of the Lord when you take your hands off of it and lean on him! No matter if you have been rejected or who don't believe in the promise...God will deal with those that are not obedient and those that question him, in the meantime, you just move forward and rest in his presence and continue doing what he has called you to do.

Preview of New Book!

"I Know What God Said Part 2"

The water was rising higher and higher and Calise was finding it hard to breathe. She panted with every lap that she made, but she was determined to make it to the shore. The wreck happened just like a dream. One minute she,

Josiah, and Adrian were riding along singing gospel to the radio, then the next minute they were slamming into the railing of a

bridge. They were traveling to Louisiana for the weekend but didn't know that this was going to happen. Calise tried not to panic. She thought about her baby and her husband. She fought back the tears that were threatening to spill down her cheeks. Just then she felt a strong tug on the back of her leg. She turned alarmed with all her might and saw her husband behind her holding Adrian in tow. Her little body lay limp against Josiah. Calise struggled against the weight of her husband, trying not to panic but it was hard. She began to pray in her spirit to the Lord. "Lord please, please, please!" She screamed out in her spirit, "Lord please save my family!!!" Just then, a swarm of lifeguards came toward them. Hope and faith flooded through Calise at that moment. Josiah held on to her feet, the lifeguards came and took each one of them and swam to the surface that was very near to them. When they got to the surface, they all laid out on the banks to catch their breath. The water came out of Calise lungs in a whoosh. Josiah looked over to Calise and asked: "Are you okay?" She managed to shake her head up and down. The two immediately began to focus on their daughter…The

paramedics worked on her. At that moment they couldn't get a pulse. Calise begin to panic. Josiah gripped her tightly and whispered "Without faith its impossible to please him." The two then joined together and began to pray and plead the blood of Jesus over their child. Just then, Adrian began to cough and water escaped her lungs. They both began to thank and praise God… ***Look for part 2 of this book coming soon!!!***

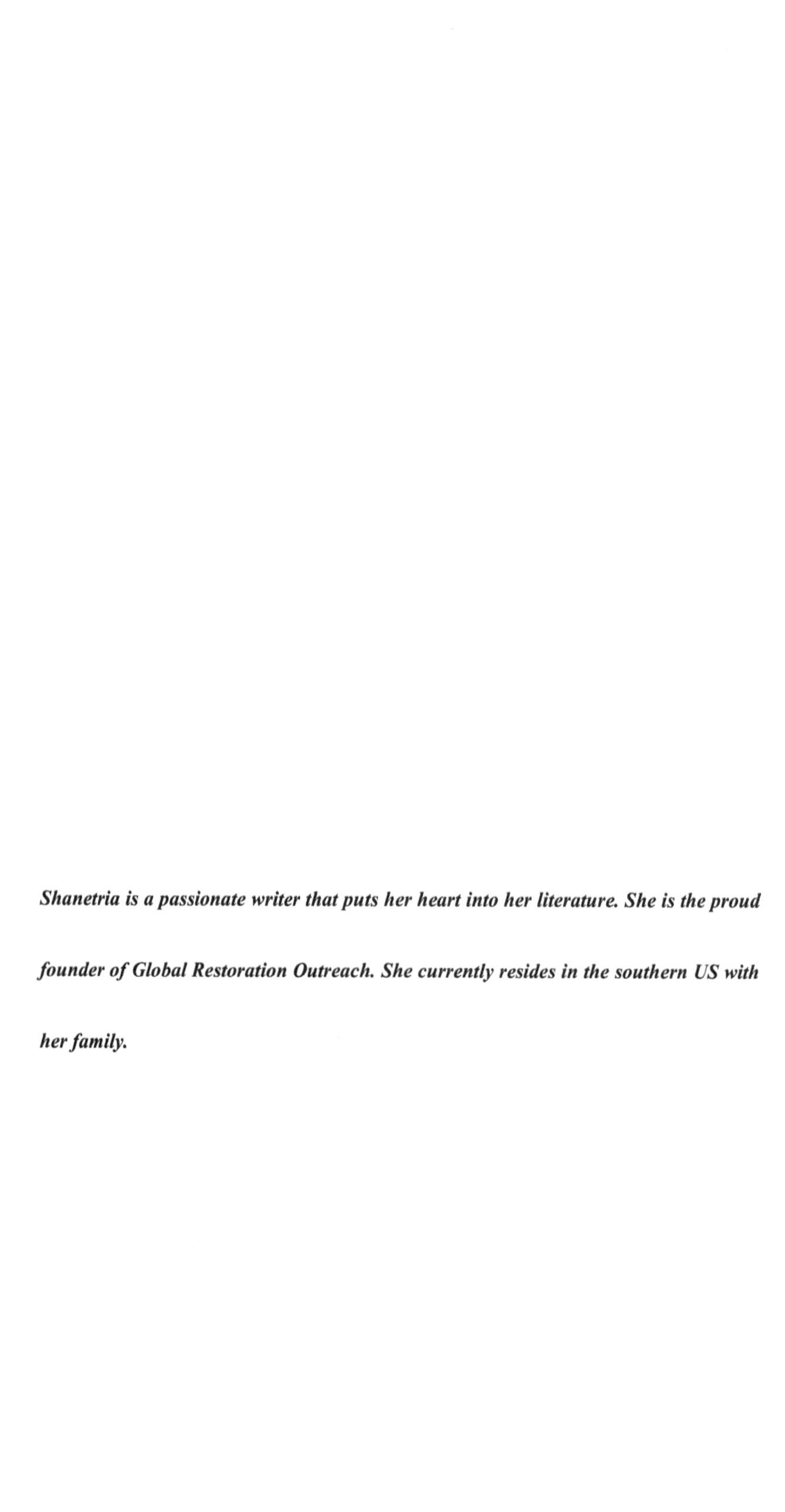

Shanetria is a passionate writer that puts her heart into her literature. She is the proud founder of Global Restoration Outreach. She currently resides in the southern US with her family.

www.ingramcontent.com/pod-product-compliance
Lightning Source LLC
Chambersburg PA
CBHW030344310726
48979CB00001B/176